Waltham Forest Libraries

Please return this item by the last date stamped. The loan may be renewed unless required by another customer.

Need to renew your books?
http://www.walthamforest.gov.uk/libraries or
Dial 0333 370 4700 for Callpoint – our 24/7 automated telephone renewal
You will need your library card number and your PIN. If you do not
r PIN, contact your local library.

Maya's Walk

Written by
Moira Butterfield

Illustrated by
Kim Geyer

OXFORD
UNIVERSITY PRESS

We *love* walking.

Which walk will we
choose today?

Are we ready?

Let's go!

We can look for tiny secrets . . .

A hole a caterpillar made
by munching on a juicy leaf.

Busy ants scurrying past.
Where are you going, little ants?

Baby plants sprouting up.
Good luck, plants.
Grow **BIG** and *Strong!*

We can feel things with our fingers . . .

A round pebble that's **smooth** and **cool**,
like an egg that's made of stone.

The lines between the bricks on walls, gritty and rough like little roads.

The tips of tall feathery grasses swaying in the breeze . . .

swish

Birds singing.
Bells ringing.
Dogs barking . . .

ruff, ruff!

People chatting.

Chitter-chat-chat

about this and that.

We can jump over
lines we find . . .

Hop-hop-hopping.

Two.

One.

Three . . .

Dancing, prancing
down the path, singing
and clapping to our beat.

We can copy animals . . .

Follow me!

Quack, quack!

Creeping cats.
Buzzing bees.

What other animals could we be?

We can spot things high above . . .

Birds sitting on a wire,
fluffing their *feathers* in a row.

A window high up in a roof.
Who lives there?
We'll make a guess.

Clouds scudding across the sky.
If they drop raindrops we won't mind.
After rain, we might get . . .

We can find some rainbow colours . . .

yellow

red

orange

blue

indigo

green

violet

We can sniff out lovely smells . . .

A blade of grass
rubbed in your hand.
A flower that has a perfume scent.

Soil that smells of earthy goodness,

a warm place for worms to live.

Whatever we decide to do,
    the very best walks are **walks with you!**

When it's time to go to bed, which walk will you dream of?

Next time we go outside,
which walk shall we try?

Shut your eyes and
wiggle your finger.
Point to the page
and choose for us.

look
for tiny
secrets

feel
with your
fingers

sniff
out lovely
smells

listen
out for
noises

spot
things high
above

jump
and hop
and
dance

copy
animals

find
rainbow
colours

OXFORD
UNIVERSITY PRESS

Great Clarendon Street, Oxford OX2 6DP

Oxford University Press is a department of the University of Oxford.
It furthers the University's objective of excellence in research, scholarship,
and education by publishing worldwide. Oxford is a registered trade mark
of Oxford University Press in the UK and in certain other countries

Text © Moira Butterfield 2022
Illustrations © Kim Geyer 2022

The moral rights of the author and illustrator have been asserted
Database right Oxford University Press (maker)

First published 2022

British Library Cataloguing in Publication Data

Data available

ISBN: 978-0-19-277853-6

1 3 5 7 9 10 8 6 4 2

Printed in China

Paper used in the production of this book is a natural, recyclable
product made from wood grown in sustainable forests. The manufacturing
process conforms to the environmental regulations
of the country of origin

For Ian, Jack and Angus (M.B.)

For Tim, Amy, Darcy and Elsa —
hopping and skipping all the way! (K.G.)